FRÉDOU

FRÉDOU

by MARY STOLZ

Pictures by TOMI UNGERER

HARPER & ROW, PUBLISHERS, NEW YORK AND EVANSTON

FOR ANNE SEIF

FRÉDOU

ONE

Early on a sunny, blue, summer morning in Paris, Frédou stood at the door of the Hotel Montvert, waving his plumy tail, surveying the street. Everything was fine. Everything, he found, was as it should be.

The fruit man at the corner sprinkled his green and dark blue grapes with a watering can. He hung a great cluster of brown-speckled, bright yellow bananas from the roof of his cart. He piled his round, ruby-red apples in a pyramid beside a cone of misty purple plums. Then he stood back, hands behind him, to see how his fruits glistened and shone.

"Very good," he said, and sat on a canvas chair beside his cart. "Ah, *bonjour*," he called, spying Frédou at the hotel entrance. "A very fine morning, is it not?"

Frédou waved his tail. The fruit man opened his newspaper and began to read.

The owner of the Turkish bakery across the street came out and let down a striped awning. "*Bonjour*, Monsieur Frédou, *bonjour*," he called, and looked at the sky and smiled, for it was indeed a fine, fine morning. He went back in his shop to arrange his strange, delicious Turkish cakes and candies so that they would be most tempting to buyers.

The flower seller wheeled her barrow into place.

2

She, too, had her little canvas chair, and she sat knitting, with mimosa and marguerites at her side and buckets of roses at her feet.

The peddler set off with a pile of rugs over one arm and a tray of silver earrings in his hands. He had golden hoops in his own ears, and an orange sash around his waist. He bowed as he passed Frédou and then continued on his way to the cafés near the Seine, where perhaps some early morning customer would see a ring or a rug that took his fancy, and buy.

Up and down the street store owners and stall owners—early risers, every one—set about their business, and Frédou, the earliest riser of all, watched from his door.

Presently, Monsieur Picot, the hotel concierge, came out and folded his arms to stand beside Frédou, looking up and down the street. Monsieur Picot wore a striped apron tied in front, and an elegant curved mustache. He had no hair on his head, but his mustaches were full and fine, of a beautiful pale apricot color. Just the shade, as the Turkish baker had once observed, of Frédou's beautiful fur.

"One might take you for relatives," the baker had said admiringly.

"Would that we were," replied Monsieur Picot, turning out his hands and lifting his eyes heavenward.

"Ah, yes," the baker had said, nodding his head with rapid understanding. "Indeed, yes."

"Frédou," said Monsieur Picot now, "today we have some American guests arriving." He took a slip of paper from his pocket and consulted it. "Monsieur and Madame Roberts, and their little boy, Paul. He is an American photographer, Monsieur Roberts. Perhaps he will take a handsome picture of me." He thought a bit and added, "Of you and me together."

"What's that, monsieur? What are you saying?" Madame Picot emerged from the shadows of the lobby into the bright sunshine at the door. She

4

wore a black dress with beads at the throat, and a pagoda of yellow hair with a long green pencil stuck through it. "What are you saying, monsieur?" she asked again.

"I was just remarking to Frédou that possibly Monsieur Roberts, the American photographer who arrives today with his wife and little boy, will take a picture of the three of us here at the entrance to the hotel."

Madame Picot smiled widely. "Oh, very good," she said. "That would be excellent. We can hang it in the lobby for everyone to look at. Now, let me see. Do you think on the wall above the spider fern, where one can see it as he enters? Or opposite the desk, where those coming down in the elevator can see it?"

"I, myself, think it would be best hung in the parlor," said the concierge. "That way, people sitting down can study it at their ease."

While Monsieur and Madame Picot discussed where they would put the picture that had not

been taken by the photographer who had not arrived, Frédou left them to go on his morning tour
of inspection.

The black and white tile of the lobby floor was
cool to his paws and admirably clean. On the desk
a pottery bowl of cosmos were bright in the gloom.
The little elevator in its open-lacework frame
waited at attention, with the stairway going around
it like a snail.

Frédou brushed past a brown and green striped
jardiniere that held the spider fern and pushed
through a curtain of wooden beads into the parlor.

Here, too, it was pleasantly shady, with draperies
drawn against the onslaught of the sun, and all the
furniture settled plumply and solidly on the flow-
ered rug.

Frédou paused a moment in this peaceful place
to settle a rumpled bit of fur on his shoulder and
smooth his whiskers nicely before continuing to
the kitchen, where the cook, who was singing of a
shepherd on a hilltop, left off and cried, "Ah, good

morning, good morning, my fine Monsieur
Frédou."

Cheerily she tossed a roll of dough in the air, let
it fall with a thump on the floury surface of her big
wooden table.

"And how is monsieur this morning?" she asked.
"Bien? Pas bien?"

Frédou sniffed the air delicately, leaned against
the cook's legs in a companionable way while she
kneaded the dough with her knuckles and talked
in a jolly, careless way, as if Frédou had come in
merely for conversation.

At length, he began to bat her ankle rapidly with
an imperious paw.

"What's this? What's this, Monsieur le Proprié-
taire?" said the cook. "What have you on your
mind now? A game of tag? Good." She leaned over
and tapped his tail. "You're It!"

Frédou moved haughtily away and stared at the
icebox with his gold-flecked eyes. Then he stared at
the cook, then at the icebox once more.

The cook slapped her thigh and gave a ringing laugh.

"Ah, monsieur," she said, "you have too much dignity to take a joke. Which is a very great pity for you," she added, being a woman who liked to give or take a joke at any time of day. "Very well, Monsieur Solemn, I will serve your breakfast in the backyard, where my frivolity won't trouble you, and your long face won't trouble me."

She took from the icebox a blue and silver fish, and led the way through the kitchen door into the backyard.

"*Voilà*," she said, and with a flourish put the fish on a bright tile table with rusted legs. "*Bon appétit.*" And she went back to the kitchen, singing of the shepherd and his sheep on the side of the hill.

Frédou leaped lightly to the table and settled on the smooth tile, paws tucked in, tail curved against his side, eyes half-closed, the fish glinting beside him.

He was not greedy, this Frédou. He merely had a strong sense of what was due him, and at this hour what was due him was a fish.

He sat alongside it, taking his time. That great Madame Bobo of a cook would see how a creature of restraint behaved at breakfast. Madame Bobo, like all noisy, cheery individuals—animal or human—vexed the very soul of the cat Frédou. He sat in the sun on the bright warm tiles and dreamed of a place absolutely silken with silence, a place where the utter stillness would be broken only once in a while, and only by moonlight, and only by the glorious shrieks and screams of cats challenging and summoning one another.

In a little while, seemingly from nowhere, and quiet as an eyelid closing, there appeared a thin young tomcat, gray as rain. He glided around a great wooden tub of soaking blue denims that reflected the sky, avoided a runnel of soapy water, and slunk to within a foot or two of the rusting table legs, where he crouched, long-bodied, staring up at the fish of Frédou with round and covetous eyes.

For a moment Frédou affected not to see. He averted his head and seemed to dream. The young tomcat grew bold, lifted on his hind legs, and with a gesture deft and swift, hooked the fish's tail with his claws and tugged . . . to find that Frédou, matching his speed, had the fish firmly secured by the gills.

They faced each other, ears down, heads flattened to the likeness of cobras, lips curled back,

noses deeply furrowed. A thin hungry growl issued from the throat of the young gray tomcat. A deep confident answer came from Frédou, a tomcat in his prime, and his pride.

"Nameless One," said Frédou, "unclaw my fish."

The gray cat snarled and tightened his grip.

With the air of a general about to level a subaltern, Frédou lifted the fur of his back in a ridge and coiled for the spring. The young gray released his hold on the fish's tail and retreated a few feet, stiff-legged, tail lashing. He lifted the fur all over his body till he seemed twice his size, but even then was only half that of Frédou. Slowly, never removing his green and glittering gaze from the face of his enemy, the gray cat weaved toward the alleyway.

All at once, Frédou changed his mind. His fur subsided. His ears lifted, displaying again their fringy beauty. His needle-taut whiskers relaxed gracefully, and the furrows departed his nose. He looked amiable, even kindly, and he said to the Nameless One, "After all, I'm not hungry. You may have the fish."

The gray cat hesitated, suspicion in every ounce of his starved body.

"No, no," said Frédou. "No tricks. The fish is yours."

"Why?" the gray cat asked, coming closer, ready to run or fight at the flick of a tail tip.

"I told you, I'm not hungry." Frédou yawned a wide, pink, lazy yawn. "For some reason, they give me all I want to eat at this hotel. It's why I remain, though the human being I liked, who lived here and doted on me in a sensible way, is gone. Dead, no doubt."

The gray, to whom death was familiar in spite of his very short life, made no answer. The death of a human being did not concern him. Nor did living humans have any part in his existence. He'd been born in a cellar to a wild and feckless mother who had never known the touch of a human hand, nor had a bite of food at one, nor had even so much as turned her head at the, "psst, *kitty, kitty*," that some humans used for no reason to any stray cat they saw.

"They feed you here?" he said, going straight to the essential point.

"Oh, but I assure you, they will not feed you. All their cat-interest centers on me. As I say, I don't understand it, but one doesn't *leave* under such circumstances."

"No," said the gray cat, lashing his tail. "No. Pride, of course, is not a factor."

Frédou, who could also get to the point, said, "Are you too proud to take this fish?"

The gray licked his chops, advanced warily, alert for treachery. His eyeballs gleamed as they rested for an instant on the fish before returning to fix the bland gaze of Frédou. Then, swift as a serpent striking, he hooked the fish, caught it in his teeth, fled to the alleyway, and was gone.

Madame Bobo, who had come to the kitchen door to empty a pail at just that moment, threw

15

back her head and roared with laughter. "Oh, he fooled you, that one, all right. Who'd ever think a gray skeleton like that one could diddle the great Frédou?"

Frédou, who understood some human words, like *bonjour*, *scat*, and the names he heard most often, had only a vague notion of what she was saying. He knew well enough what laughter was, and ordinarily resented it. Not today. He tucked in his paws and settled on the tiles to sleep.

He was not by any means finished with the gray and nameless cat, but he could do something few humans could do, and that was to bide his time.

TWO

Mr. and Mrs. Roberts and their son, Paul, were coming from the airport, Orly, in a square black taxi with a driver who wore a soft peaked cap and had a cigarette behind his ear. He whistled and drove with a great deal of dash.

"Isn't this exciting, Paul?" Mrs. Roberts said to her son. "See how they have their food markets out on the sidewalk? And, oh, look at the beautiful flower market! Just look at those vegetables. And the oyster man. And look, Paul, see the little tables outside the cafés? One day we will go to a café and you shall have a citronnade. That's French for lemonade," she explained, and clutched her husband's arm. "Isn't that the Arc de Triomphe, right there, ahead, ahead—"

Paul, who had not spoken a word since they landed at Orly, did not speak one now. His mother could get as excited as she wanted about markets and oysters and arks de tree-whatever-it-was, but all Paul wanted was to be back home. He wanted it so badly that he squeezed his eyes shut and thought so hard he almost *felt* back—

Where his friends were playing on the beach, hurling themselves in the big waves, building fortresses and the palaces in the wet sand, running in the sun beside the pounding water. Back with Aladdin. . .

His eyes flew open, and here he was, of course, tearing along a strange road, with signs in a language he couldn't read, and people who lived here all the time going about as if it was perfectly all right to be in Paris, France, and not on Long Island.

Which, he said to himself, grimly determined to be fair, it is. For them. For Paul Roberts, to be here was awful. He thought about Aladdin, black and shining as a seal, dashing into the waves and barking louder than ten other dogs put together. He set his jaw and thought of Turkey Hoffman, running along with Aladdin, and calling to him, and *being* with him.

Unless, he thought, it's night over there now. He believed it probably was.

"When it is nighttime here," his teacher had told the class, "it is daytime in the lands across the ocean."

Here he was, across the ocean, in the daytime, so Aladdin and Turkey Hoffman were not on the

beach but inside, maybe sleeping. Aladdin, sleeping in Turkey's room, as if he belonged there. But
the morning would come, and all his friends would
wake up, and Aladdin and Turkey, too, and they'd
run down to the beach and be there all day, while
Paul went to a city where he had no friends and
didn't know what anyone was saying.

He sat between his mother and his father while
they cried out, "See this, look at that, oh, do look
over there," and didn't seem to notice that he said
nothing in reply, and that his eyes were too blurred
for him to see anything at all.

After a long time the taxi pulled up before a
small hotel on a very narrow street. The driver took
the cigarette from behind his ear and lit it. He
tossed over his shoulder a stream of words in
French, to which Mr. Roberts replied slowly, but
in French also.

Paul huddled back and let everything take place
around him and wished he hadn't gotten too old to
cry.

The luggage was removed from the roof of the cab and piled on the street.

A bald man wearing a striped apron and a big smile under his curling mustaches emerged from the hotel, followed by a lady with a great pile of yellow hair held together with a pencil, followed by a large, lazy-looking cat with long silky fur the color of the man's mustaches.

Paul brightened a little when he saw the cat, but it turned away with such a look of boredom that he felt insulted.

He squeezed his eyes shut again and pushed against the back of the taxi seat, wishing he'd wake up and find that Paris was a dream he didn't have to have any more.

"Come along, Paul," said his father, reaching in a hand to help him out. Paul tugged back and felt his father's grip tighten. "Come out and meet Monsieur and Madame Picot."

Slowly Paul inched his way to the sidewalk, then stood before Monsieur and Madame Picot with his eyes cast down, knowing that as soon as he was alone with his mother she was going to say a whole lot of things about manners.

"Paul," said Mrs. Roberts, in a soft warning tone. "Paul, please say hello to Monsieur and Madame Picot."

I will *not* say hello to them, Paul told himself. I won't say anything to them at all. I'm not going to say hello to anybody the whole rest of this summer. He planted his feet apart, and stubbornness rose in him like a wave coming up the beach.

"Paul?" said his father, not quite sharply. It was a familiar sound, his father deciding to make sure he did what his mother had asked. For a moment it carried Paul back home, and he said, almost happily, "Hello, Mon—Mon— Mr. and Mrs. Picot."

He lifted his gaze to the couple standing before him. The woman had eyes as dark and shiny as the beads around her neck, and her yellow hair went up and up like a frozen custard. She bobbed her head, and did not smile.

But Monsieur Picot bent down so that his face was on a level with Paul's.

"'Allo, 'allo, 'allo," he said, very quickly. He looked like a nice little walrus, and in spite of himself, Paul smiled.

"I didn't know anyone spoke English," he said. "I mean, I don't speak French."

"Ah, but by the time the summer is over, little man, you will, you will," said the walrus.

Paul, who did not like being called little man, glanced away without replying. The summer, he thought. The whole long summer. It was half gone now. By the time he got home, it would be over, and all his friends gone from the beach, and the ocean cold, and their own house—which they had rented to some people for the season—boarded up, empty. He wouldn't see the beach again for a *year*.

"Monsieur Picot," said Mr. Roberts, "we are most eager to meet Monsieur Frédou. The friend who recommended your hotel to us said we must meet Monsieur Frédou, the owner, as soon as we

arrived. He says Monsieur Frédou is a most un-
usual fellow."

"Ah, true, true," said Monsieur Picot with a
broad and beaming smile. "That he is. I am most
happy to introduce you. Monsieur Frédou," he
said, "I should like you to make the acquaintance

of Monsieur and Madame Roberts, from Long Island, America, and their son, Paul."

Mr. and Mrs. Roberts, and Paul, too, looked all around in great curiosity, for there was no one besides themselves at the hotel entrance. Then Paul saw that Monsieur Picot was gesturing toward the great proud cat, who, at the word Frédou, leaped to the window ledge and studied the newcomers.

"But it can't be," said Mrs. Roberts. "The cat? You are having a joke with us, monsieur."

"Far from it," said Monsieur Picot. "You see before you Monsieur Frédou, owner and proprietor of this hotel."

THREE

At home, elevators were closed up in the wall, like closets. But Paul found the elevators here right out in the open, surrounded by lacy-looking grillwork. The elevator itself was like a bird cage going up and down within the grillwork and a little stairway went winding around outside.

There was room in the little cage for only three

people at a time, so Paul waited while Monsieur Picot took his mother and father up to inspect the rooms. He watched as they slowly ascended, and when their feet had disappeared from view, sighed and sat on a suitcase.

Madame Picot said something he didn't understand and went away, leaving the curtain of wooden beads swaying and clicking behind her. Paul watched until the strings of beads hung quite straight and still. He'd never seen anything like that before, either.

He put his chin on his hands, elbows on his knees, and tried to stop thinking about anything. Idly, he glanced out the front door and saw that great cat, Frédou, start off down the street with an air of going somewhere in particular. He wondered what particular place a cat would have in mind to go to. After all, a dog, a dog like Aladdin, who was very intelligent, had a great many things on his mind that he couldn't share even with his best friend, Paul. Aladdin frequently went off on er-

rands of his own. He always came back, of course.

But a cat?

Paul decided that even if the cat looked as if he knew where he was going, probably he had no idea at all. He was just wandering, the way cats do, with nothing special in mind. Maybe he'd never find his way back. Not that Paul cared.

But it was funny, the cat owning the hotel. Monsieur Picot had explained that the former owner, when she died, left the hotel and everything in it to her cat, this Frédou.

"Providing," Monsieur Picot had said, "that he retains Madame and me as concierges, and Madame Bobo as cook, and Pierre as porter, and Yvette and Marie as upstairs maids. So far," he added happily, "nobody has been fired."

Pretty silly, Paul thought now. How could a cat fire anybody? Losing interest in the cat, he began to wonder what Aladdin was doing, now, right this minute. A feeling familiar to this summer began to hurt Paul again. It was as if a big fist was squeezing his stomach, every time he thought about his dog and Turkey Hoffman.

"Don't you worry about Aladdin for one minute," Mr. Hoffman had said. "He'll have a great time here at the beach."

Paul had had to smile, and look as if that was what he wanted. The awful truth was—though he could never, never tell this to anyone—the truth was, he didn't want Aladdin to have a great summer at the beach, playing and swimming and sleeping with Turkey Hoffman. Looking to Turkey for food and for fun and for just some talk now and then. Aladdin was the sort of dog who enjoyed just sitting and sort of listening once in a while. You could tell him anything, and he seemed to understand. Paul hadn't told Turkey about this, but Turkey would catch on. The dog had a way of looking at you that just made you tell him what was on your mind.

The awful truth was, Paul didn't want Aladdin

to have a great summer at the beach. He wanted Aladdin to be miserable, the way he was. Because suppose . . . just suppose Turkey and Aladdin . . . suppose Aladdin got so he—

Paul couldn't complete the thought. He swallowed to smooth away that feeling in his stomach, and then because it wouldn't go while he sat still, started up the stairway that wound around the elevator, pulling himself along by the railing.

On the third floor he found his parents exclaiming over how nice the rooms were, and Monsieur Picot beaming as he said that he would now go for the luggage. He got into the cage, closed the door, and started down. It was funny to see him drop out of sight that way, like a walrus sinking into the sea. Just as his head was about to disappear, he winked at Paul. By the time Paul had unwillingly winked back, it was too late, and the walrus face was gone.

"Paul," said Mrs. Roberts, "isn't this a wonderful little hotel?" She seemed very happy, and was fluttering between the big room that was for her and Paul's father, and the smaller one across the hall that was Paul's.

"Paul," she said, when he didn't answer, "don't you think it's amazing—that gorgeous cat owning the hotel?"

"I think it's silly," Paul said, half under his breath, but not low enough so that his father didn't hear him.

"Paul doesn't think anything is wonderful or amazing," Mr. Roberts said to his wife. "Haven't you noticed?"

"Of course I have," said Mrs. Roberts, looking troubled. She went into Paul's room and sat down on the bed, patting the place beside her. "Come on, dear. We'll talk it out."

Paul didn't see that there was anything to talk out. They were here. There was no help for it. There hadn't been any help for being in Rome, either, where they'd spent nearly a month. It was his father's job to take pictures, and this time the job was over here, and his parents had decided it was a fine opportunity for him to see Europe. They could have left him with his grandmother. He had *asked* them to. But here he was having the fine opportunity anyway.

Here he was in Paris, there was another month to go, and he hadn't talked to anyone his own age in weeks. So what was there to talk to his mother about?

"Now, tell me," said Mrs. Roberts. "How can we help you, dear, if you won't tell us what is wrong?"

It was peculiar that somebody who understood as much as his mother did at home should stop understanding anything at all once she got out of the country.

That first night, on the airplane, when he'd almost strangled trying to keep from crying for Aladdin, she'd thought he was afraid of the *flying*. She was so pleased and excited about going to Europe that Paul had decided not to say it wasn't the flying but the whole trip that bothered him.

He thought he'd done pretty well at not spoiling things, for the first few weeks, anyway. He'd laughed and talked with his parents, and been interested in the Roman sights—some of which *were* interesting, like the Colosseum, where the lions had eaten the Christians, and the Forum, where Caesar, of whom they'd read in school, had actually fallen, stabbed dead, and all those fountains with statues in them, and the—what was it called?—the Pantheon, where, it had seemed to Paul, hundreds, maybe thousands, of cats lived in a moat. He'd hung over that moat, staring down at the lean, fierce cats, and for the first time in his life thought that maybe a cat was all right in itself, and not just something Aladdin was interested in chasing. The cats had looked so—so sad and proud.

There'd been one misty-colored kitten that had stared up at him with eyes bright as green glass, and Paul had said to his father, "Couldn't we take one home, Dad? Maybe that one." He pointed at the glaring kitten.

"Anyone who went down in that moat," Mr. Roberts had said, "would be torn to shreds in seconds. Those aren't housecats, Paul. They're blood kin of tigers, not even once removed."

"Besides," said Mrs. Roberts, "what would Aladdin say to that? He'd never forgive you."

Paul, who understood Aladdin better than his parents ever could, thought Aladdin might be very kind to a thin and hungry kitten. Dogs, as a matter of fact, were known for their kindness to kittens. But since it was apparently hopeless to wish for that particular misty little cat, Paul lost interest. Somehow they never returned to the Pantheon, and somehow the fact that he had no one his own age to talk to began to be so important to Paul that he forgot about everything else. Except Aladdin, of course. And thinking about Aladdin was no help, since that meant he had to put Turkey Hoffman in the same thought, and Turkey spoiled everything.

Which was how it came about that, in spite of being rather good the first few weeks, Paul began, in his turn, to spoil things, too. He stopped laughing, stopped finding the sights interesting, all but stopped talking. And his mother patting the bed and saying, "Won't you tell us what's wrong, dear," was no help. He was past help, from them or himself.

He'd retreated into this silence (sulkiness, his mother called it) as an experiment, in the beginning. Not that he really thought anything he did would make his father cut short the trip and take them all home, but still—it was *just* possible. He'd even considered pretending to be sick, but his mother had caught him putting the thermometer on the light bulb, and that ended that. All he'd gotten for his pains was a long talking to from both his parents about sportsmanship and the fine opportunity he was wasting.

The sad fact was that in a way he agreed, but now couldn't come out of his silence even if he wanted to. Which he sometimes did and sometimes didn't. The experiment was a flop, but he was like a fly who'd set out to explore a web. By the time he and the fly realized that some things are better left unexplored, there was no way out.

So he sat beside his mother in this little room in Paris in the hotel owned by a cat and shook his head when she said, "What's wrong, Paul? Let us help you."

"Nothing is," he said at length. "I just don't feel like talking."

With an exasperated sound, his mother got to her feet. "Well," she said, looking down at her son, "your father has to go see an editor, whose office is on the Champs Elysées, and I should very much like to see the Champs Elysées."

"Go see it," Paul muttered. "What do I care?"

Mrs. Roberts hesitated. At length she said, "I think you are even more unhappy than you are rude. So there's probably no point in punishing you. Or asking you to apologize."

"I apologize," said Paul coldly.

As if she hadn't heard him, his mother went on.

"Please stay here at the hotel while we're gone. We won't be long." She went to the door, turned, and said, "If you continue this way for the entire remaining four weeks, you'll succeed in making us all very unhappy. If that's what you want. . ."

This seemed to Paul such a dumb thing to say that he didn't answer, and in a moment his mother left to go with his father and see the—the— He couldn't remember the name of the place his mother had wanted to see.

So what? he said to himself, and wandered to the window. His room was at the rear of the hotel, overlooking a courtyard, where a fat woman was sitting on a chair, shelling peas into a big white pot. A huge wooden tub of blue laundry was soaking beside her, and as Paul watched, a young girl came out and began to beat the laundry with a paddle. Accustomed to washing machines, Paul found this very interesting. He pulled a chair up to the window, sat with his chin in his hands and watched.

The girl wrung the clothes out with swift twisty movements of her hands, emptied the tub and let the soapy water run into a sort of gutter. Then she tossed the laundry back in the tub and turned a hose on it.

Golly, thought Paul, what a *hard* way to do laundry. Yet the girl seemed very cheerful. She and the fat woman talked and laughed together while they worked. At one point Monsieur Picot stepped out in the yard and joined them. He, too, laughed and gestured with his hands and seemed in fine spirits. The sight of so much cheeriness offended Paul, who looked away from them at the windows opposite. There were a great many geraniums in pots on the window sills, and people had hung bedding out to air. Jutting out at angles were tiled roofs with black squatty chimney pots and here and there on the rooftops were sunning cats. There certainly seemed to be a lot of cats in Europe. Far more than at home. Unless, Paul thought, it's that Aladdin keeps them all away.

With a tremendous sigh, he left the window and sat on his bed, staring in turn at a colored glass lampshade, a curtained wardrobe, and the floor. After a while, he lay down on the bed and just stared at the ceiling.

FOUR

Frédou turned into the Street of the Fishing Cat and, since it may be the shortest street in the world, was through it very quickly and onto the Quai St. Michel, where he strolled along, watching the bookkeepers of the Seine open their stands for business.

They called to him as he passed.

"Ah, Monsieur Frédou, and how is the capitalist this morning?" they said, in a mixture of amusement and respect. "Does old Picot work hard enough to suit your eminence? What's the situation of your mortgage? Would you trade it for a nice chicken liver, or a spoonful of caviar?"

They arranged their books, their old prints and postcards, their Roman helmets, in such a manner as to tempt passing students and tourists, and addressed Frédou waggishly as he sauntered by.

Frédou knew they were speaking to him. He waved his tail gracefully and kept walking. He enjoyed their attention, but did not propose to give them his. Human beings, clumsy and noisy enough to make a cat laugh, were all right in their place, but Frédou was no longer a pet. Nor, since that pleasingly low-voiced person with the strong and gentle hands was gone, had he any wish to be. It was excellent that he was still apparently welcome at the hotel, and that they fed him, but it seemed to him no reason for too great familiarity.

He crossed Pont St. Michel, went past the Palais du Justice, across Pont au Change, and so to the Quai de Gesvres. Here, on this street of caged and colorful birds, he was not known as Frédou, the owner of the excellent small Hotel Montvert, but as that great orange pest, upon whom all the shopkeepers kept a sharp and angry eye as he passed, alert to their wares, but helpless, of course, to buy or steal.

All up and down the Quai were the shops of seed merchants and bird sellers. Frédou sniffed the aroma pleasurably. Not that he cared for seeds in his own diet, but the associations were pleasant. Within their wooden cages, the bright-plumaged birds studied him furiously. They were not alarmed, were even thankful, though briefly, for the protection of their prisons, but they did not like to see him there, looking so free and so appreciative. It was a type of appreciation that the birds, in turn, could not appreciate.

A jet-black crow, not caged but shackled to a

stand, opened his bill wide and hissed as the cat went by, whereupon Frédou turned back and sat down to study this character more closely.

"New here, aren't you?" he said, keeping an eye on the shopkeeper who was keeping an eye on him. "Aren't you?" he repeated to the crow, who hissed again and settled down glumly on his perch, his head seeming to sink in his body.

Frédou gave his chest a couple of licks, blinked innocently at the bird above him, and said, "I never attack, you know. At least, not where I'd get caught so quickly. Anyway, hardly ever birds. Funny about people. They absolutely *want* you to go after some creatures. Rats, for instance. It occurs to me some-times that it's because of my terrible reputation among the rats of the Left Bank that I'm treated so royally at the hotel where I live. Oh, but you don't know about that, do you?"

He paused a moment, in case the crow should wish to speak, but meeting only a deep and dark-some silence, continued, "On the other hand, if

one makes a move toward a bird, especially a bird in a cage, one has the whole human race to contend with. And from time to time I am compelled by some force within me to take out after one of these powder-puff pet pooches, these mincing, yapping ladies' dogs. You should hear the squalls that result. Of all animals, I'd say the human was the most illogical."

The crow lifted his wings slightly, thrust his head forward, and hissed again. In spite of himself, Frédou backed away. He turned and continued his walk, pondering on the strangeness of life, where creatures that were made for freedom could be caged and pinioned in this fashion. It seemed to him that his crime of occasionally catching and killing a bird was far less terrible than what was done by the people who got so angry with him for doing it. Even that kindly remembered woman had become furious when he brought her a pigeon offering.

He went back across Pont de Notre Dame, turned

into the flower market, where, when no one was looking, he quickly nibbled at some bitter-sweet rose leaves, tender on the stalk. Delicious, delicious. He purred faintly as his teeth crunched the delicacy.

"Hi, you orange devil, scaat!"

A shower of water rained on his fur and he fled to the safety of a nearby alley. Here he stopped and attended to his wet and rumpled fur, his pink rough tongue catching occasionally in the luxuriant hairs so that he had to shake his head loose before continuing.

Think of it. All that fury for the loss of a few tiny rose leaves, which actually were not entirely lost at all. Just slightly chewed. Oh, but how sweet they were, how dainty a treat, those rose leaves—

He walked on, keeping to the alleyways and back courtyards now. Too bad the crow hadn't felt conversational. Frédou, who was curious about all creatures, would very much have liked to hear of the crow's life, of what had brought him to this pass, and whether he planned an escape, as Frédou in that position would most certainly have been doing.

But that was the way it went. He was curious to a point of mania, this Frédou, but scarcely ever found another animal curious enough about him to indulge in an exchange of memories and desire. He'd even tried with the rats, who, after all, had been to sea, many of them. Or at any rate had sailed the barges up and down the Seine. But the rats simmered at him evilly and turned tail and ran, every time.

Horrible things, rats. Those thin, long, hairless tails. It wasn't fair, of course, to judge a creature by its tail, still Frédou often fell into the sin of doing so. He numbered several squirrels among his acquaintance, and it was in good measure because of their flicky, flirty tails that he never made an aggressive gesture toward them. They were, of course, rather big and rowdy game for a cat even of Frédou's size, but it was mostly for admiration of their tails that he kept his claws to himself in their company.

Still, the squirrels never saw much more of life than he did himself, so conversation with them was really more chat and gossip than information.

He was on his way now, through alleys and courtyards, to a certain old and elegant house near Pont d'Arcole, where lived the beautiful Thomasine, a Siamese with fur like cream and caramel, and eyes

bluer than the Paris sky. Since he had encountered her on his morning walk a few weeks ago, Frédou had fancied this Thomasine above all he'd ever known. She was a traveled cat, talkative and entertaining, with a deliciously vibrating voice and a dark, sinuous tail. With all the ardor of his wild cat being, Frédou wanted Thomasine to come to the Left Bank and live at his hotel with him forever. He wanted to share his morning fish with her, and his daily prowls, and his nighttime roistering along the roofs and fences of the town. It baffled him almost to madness that he, the splendid Frédou, with all he had to offer, had gotten nowhere at all in this courtship.

Thomasine appeared glad to see him arrive, pleased to see him go. She talked with him, played with him, left him without notice, reappeared without a sound, and greeted with a pink-tongued laugh his proposals that she leave this household with its overpowering mistress, its too cat-loving master, its tiresome spaniel dog, and come with him to a place where human beings kept their place and dogs were not permitted.

Patience and persistence were qualities Frédou possessed totally, and so he came here once, twice, sometimes three times daily, in order to see and talk with Thomasine, in order to woo her.

He turned now into a courtyard quite different —he had to admit much finer—than the courtyard of the Hotel Montvert. Here trees and bushes and flowers filled the warm air with rustling fragrance. Vines fluttered against the walls, and a little fountain splashed above a small deep pool. Small and canny carp swam in the depths of this pool, always out of paw-reach, though in any case Thomasine had made it clear on his first day's visit that the carp were not for catching.

"What are they for, then?" Frédou had asked.

"Decoration," said Thomasine. *"They* set great store by this fountain and pool. The fish are part of it."

Frédou had peered into the shining depths at

the slow-moving gape-eyed fish with their ever-moving mouths pushing around for food. Not, he would have thought, very decorative. But *They*, in common with other humans, had odd ideas of attractiveness. You couldn't fault them altogether, since they cherished Thomasine. On the other hand, there were these unlovely fish unreasonably protected, and there was that spaniel dog, Drummer, whose odious presence could be detected even when he was absent. He had a peculiar smell compounded of dog and soap (he submitted to *baths*) that troubled Frédou's nostrils. And his voice! And his blundering, undignified manner!

"How do you stand him?" Frédou had asked the delicate Thomasine.

"I grew up with him," she said, as if that explained everything, or anything.

Coming into the courtyard now, alert for Thomasine, Frédou saw with impatience that the lean and hungry gray, looking less lean and hungry for Frédou's own fish, was curled on a low tile rooftop jutting out over the kitchen. Thomasine was on a window sill above, gazing down at him with a fond and anxious look in her great blue eyes. It was a manner in which she never looked upon Frédou, and he suspected it was because he looked neither underfed nor over-timid.

Spying Frédou, the gray began to back up the roof, ears down, turning his head this way and that, as though seeking an escape. As though, Frédou thought scornfully, terrified of a pitiless enemy. I, said the big cat, silently watching the small cat cower away, *I* who only a few hours ago *gave* him my breakfast.

Oh, he knew well enough what the Nameless One had in mind with this behavior. To win, even more than he had already won, the tender regard of Thomasine, a cat who had probably lived too long with human beings and so was subject to sentimentality.

When the gray cat had slunk from sight, Thomasine turned her wide blue gaze down on Frédou, and said coldly, "Are you satisfied, you bully? Frightening a poor thin creature half your size?"

Too proud to defend himself, Frédou returned her glance. His own was full of admiration. Really, she was a most beautiful cat. He valued her above oysters, and intended, no matter how, to win her.

FIVE

Paul and his mother were having a citronnade at a café near the Cathedral of Notre Dame. Paul, at the moment, was not drinking. He had his hands in his pockets, and was kicking his heels on the sidewalk, staring at the great church across the street, half listening to his mother talk about it.

". . . nearly three hundred years to build," Mrs.

Roberts was saying, "and every stone put in place by hand. The carvings and gargoyles were done by hand, also, of course. We'll go over after a while and look at the portals, shall we, and the stained-glass windows. Some of them—the great rose window, for instance—are over seven hundred years old." She looked at her son and said, "Don't you want your lemonade?"

"Oh, sure," said Paul. He leaned forward and took a little sip, still with his hands in his pockets, then slumped back, balancing one foot on the toe of the other.

A bee came buzzing over the table, a little, slender, black and yellow bee. It hovered above a spilled drop of citronnade on the tabletop, circled, landed, and began delicately to drink from the drop. Paul watched its tiny head dip up and down, and smiled a little.

"Heaven send us more bees," said Mrs. Roberts, "if that's what it takes to make you smile."

Things were getting worse. There was no ques-

tion of that. They'd been in Paris a week now, and it was getting harder and harder for Mrs. Roberts to pretend they were having fun. Mr. Roberts, of course, was frequently away on business, photographing the people and places of France. Today he was in Marseilles, but was due back in the morning, when they were all supposed to drive to Versailles together.

Suddenly Paul looked up at his mother. "This . . . Versailles—" he said, and stopped.

"Yes, Paul? What about it?"

"I don't want to go."

"Oh." There was a very long silence, and then Mrs. Roberts said, "All right. Your father can go alone." She didn't sound angry, only sad.

"Why can't you go with him?" Paul asked.

"And leave you?"

"Why not? I'll be fine at the hotel. My gosh, it's only for a couple of days. I should think maybe you'd like to get away from me for a bit. I know I would," he added grumpily.

Mrs. Roberts' lips curved a little. "You wouldn't, perhaps, feel that way if you'd make an effort to enjoy things. It's because you're so . . . so—"

"Sulky," Paul supplied.

"Well, you are, dear. Very. And it isn't as if you were going to change anything with your attitude. Your father has to finish up here, and it can't be before the end of the month, and we're sorry we didn't know how *much* you hated coming with us—"

"It isn't that at all," Paul interrupted hotly. "That's not fair. I only . . . only didn't want to leave home."

"Well, no matter how you put it, it's like rain on the picnic, being with you."

Paul straightened a little. Actually, he preferred to be talked to this way than to have them always trying to coax him into enjoying things he did not enjoy, or having little talks with him that didn't get anyone anywhere.

And he did have a feeling that if they went away

for a couple of days, if he could be alone for a bit, he could maybe work his way out of this mood. Sometimes at home, when school or the constant presence of people or just *things* got to be too much, he would go off for a walk with Aladdin (who was so much a part of him that it was like being alone) and when he got back everything would be somehow easier. The arithmetic problems would turn out to have answers after all, the people would be nice to be with once again, and *things* would either be all right or not matter.

If it worked at home, maybe it would work here. Except for no Aladdin. Well, maybe he could pretend Aladdin was along.

A couple of times in the last few days he'd had the most peculiar feeling about that big cat, Frédou. It was as if Frédou, setting out on those morning jaunts of his, was actually inviting Paul to go along. He'd linger at Paul's side, looking at him with those steady gleaming yellow eyes, and then stroll away a little, and then look back as if to say,

"Well, are you coming?" Paul had almost gone along once, and then decided he was being crazy. Whoever heard of a cat inviting a person for a walk?

On the other hand, was it impossible? Why shouldn't a cat, especially one practically as big as a dog, with a hotel to boot and probably money in the bank, enjoy a bit of company on his walk? Like Mr. Ross, the banker back home.

Well, if his parents decided to go to Versailles without him, he'd find out. He'd just take that old cat up on the invitation and see what happened. Probably the cat would slope off at the first turning and leave Paul stranded somewhere, but he wasn't especially alarmed about that. He'd been lost before. Not in Paris, of course. But he'd discovered that practically all Parisian policemen speak English, so it was the same thing as getting lost at home. You could practically enjoy it, knowing that at any minute a policeman could tell you where you were and how to get back where you wanted to be.

"I don't know," Mrs. Roberts was saying doubtfully. "Suppose something went wrong?"

"Why should something go wrong?" Paul asked. "Don't you think I'm *old* enough to stay by myself?"

"Of course I do. For a while, anyway. Besides, there's a hotel full of people, so you wouldn't precisely be by yourself."

"Well then?" said Paul, knowing his mother was weakening. Probably she really did want to get away from him. Probably she and his father would have a great old time, just being together, without their son trailing along like a storm warning. And Paul didn't blame them. But how could you smile when everybody was saying all the time, *"Paul, please smile"*?

He really did hope they'd decide to leave him for a bit. He felt sort of guilty about wishing this, but wished it just the same.

"Well, if it's all right with your father," Mrs. Roberts was saying, "we can speak to the Picots.

I'm sure they wouldn't mind looking out for you for a couple of days."

Paul started to say he didn't need anyone looking out for him, then decided it would be wiser to say nothing. If somebody didn't agree to, his mother would never go.

"Monsieur Picot will say yes," he said confidently.

"I'm sure he would," Mrs. Roberts agreed. "He does seem to like you."

It was true. Monsieur Picot appeared to find Paul enchanting. "He is the grouchiest little boy I have ever known," Monsieur Picot would say, as if it were a virtue on Paul's part. "I have never seen anything like it before. Never, never." He had taken Paul all over the hotel, introducing him to people, apparently proud of this prodigy of a grouch. Madame Picot, on the other hand, almost never spoke to Paul, which was all right with him but annoyed his mother.

Mothers are nice, Paul thought now. Always

looking out for you. Even if you didn't want to be looked out for, it was nice of them. Maybe Aladdin sometimes felt this way about Paul himself? This was a new thought, and he turned it over carefully. Those times when Aladdin went off by himself . . . maybe he wasn't going *to* someplace, but just *away* from someplace? Maybe everything—people, animals, even that bee drinking the citronnade—wanted to be alone sometimes, away from the other people and animals and bees. But, in that case, he didn't have to feel guilty about wishing his parents would go to Versailles without him, he just had to hope they would go.

They did. Mr. Roberts didn't even hesitate as long as his wife had. He found it a splendid idea and said so immediately, causing Paul an unexpected qualm. Was he really as bad as all that, that his father could hardly even wait to get away? He tried to pretend he was his father, and that his own son Paul was behaving . . . behaving how? Paul frowned. Well, he didn't want to be here, but he'd told them that, so it wasn't his fault if he was cross. Was it? No . . . no, it was not. He was here against his will, and that entitled him to be cross. Didn't it?

The next day, after his parents had driven off, he sat at the window with his chin on his fists, and argued back and forth with himself about whether or not he had a right to be cross.

He was grateful after a while to see Madame Bobo, shiny as an apple, coming out of the kitchen door down in the courtyard. It gave him a chance to stop thinking about himself. Madame Bobo, with Frédou stepping neatly at her heels, crossed to the tile table that was always out in rain or shine, and put on it the fish she was carrying. Then she gestured for Frédou to partake.

He leaped up on the table but made no move to eat, and Madame Bobo stood for a few minutes, hands on her hips, talking to him in gunfire French. She had no English at all, but a marvelous smile that Mr. Roberts said was a language in itself. Since she scarcely ever left her kitchen, and Paul

had been there only once, they were hardly acquainted. But he liked her, and often watched her from his window here. He also liked Pierre and Yvette and Marie, who worked so hard and always seemed to be in such sunny spirits. The trouble was that the brighter they were, the sulkier Paul seemed, and he supposed that by now nobody thought he liked anybody.

But there he was, thinking about himself again. He shook his head and concentrated on Frédou, who seemed to be concentrating on nothing. Paws tucked in, tail at his side, statue-still beside his fish, he simply sat in the sun. And now, from the alley-

way, creeping slowly, came a thin cat, a mist-gray cat, with green eyes fixed steadily on the fish of Frédou. Slowly, slowly he advanced, and Paul found himself holding his breath. Frédou seemed unaware. He stared into nothingness, not a whisker moving, and the small gray cat came closer, closer, soft and cautious as a burglar stepping in his stocking feet. Then, in a sudden dash, he made it to the table, hooked the fish in his paw, carried it to his mouth and turned, all in a single-seeming gesture. Like a streak of rain running down a glass pane he flowed across the courtyard and was gone.

Paul burst out laughing. It had been a most daring robbery. Right in broad daylight, right under the eyes of Frédou. Somehow that thin gray cat reminded Paul of the kitten in the Pantheon, the kitten he still wondered about and thought of as his and Aladdin's. This one was older, of course. But as thin. As hungry, he guessed. Certainly as tough and wild. It would take a *very* tough cat to steal from that great Frédou, who even now did

not seem ready to fight for his fish. He only turned his head in the direction the thief had taken and then quite calmly began to wash his face.

Coming to a decision, Paul left his room, ran around down the stairway and straight into Madame Picot, who frowned and rearranged the pencil (a blue one today) in her cone of yellow hair.

"Oh, excuse me, Mrs. — I mean, Madame Picot," stammered Paul. "Is it all right if I go through the kitchen?"

"What for?"

"I—" It sounded pretty silly, but Paul pressed on. "I want to see if Frédou—if he wants me to go for a walk with him."

"A walk, is it? Well, one can't guess with Frédou just what it is he wants. Very well, you may go through the kitchen, if you proceed slowly."

"Oh, yes. Yes, of course, madame."

Paul went slowly through the curtain of beads, the parlor, a hallway, and so into the kitchen. Pierre, Yvette and Marie, after scrubbing, scouring, sweeping, making beds and carrying luggage since early morning were having a cup of coffee at the kitchen table. Madame Bobo was stirring vegetables into a *pot au feu* at the back of the stove.

They all stopped talking and looked at Paul when he came in. Overcome with shyness, he stood in the doorway, and wished he'd stayed in his room.

"Ah, the little grouch," Pierre said amiably.

Pierre, Yvette and Marie, who all spoke a little English, called Paul the little grouch, and it made him quite angry in spite of the fact that his father said they undoubtedly did not know the real meaning of the word and took it for some sort of pet name.

"Well, why don't you tell them differently?" Paul had demanded hotly.

"Why don't you?" said his father, and that ended that conversation.

Now Paul looked at them all smiling at him so warmly. He decided his father was right. They

75

thought they were saying something nice to him, and since they thought it, perhaps it was. Monsieur Picot, on the other hand, knew perfectly well what a grouch was, only he seemed to find it entertaining.

How peculiar things are, thought Paul, and he didn't mean only in Paris. He smiled back and said, with much daring, his very first word in French.

"*Bonjour*," he said.

Ah, how that delighted them. Astonished, Paul heard them cry out and congratulate him and one another in a mixture of French, English and laughter.

"A very good start," said Pierre, "veery good. In a little while he will be speaking finer French than all of us together, eh?"

Paul lowered his eyes in confusion. He suddenly felt very happy, and wished that he knew a lot of other words. He wished, in fact, that he could speak the whole French language, all of a sudden, just like that. That would certainly astound them. He could just fancy how they'd beat him on the back, and tell each other how clever he was. Though the fact was they were practically doing that for just *bonjour*.

I guess I'll learn French, Paul said to himself, and glanced out the window to see Frédou stretch on the tabletop, and then gaze in the window at him, as if waiting.

SIX

Because he was so big, so well taken care of, so sure of himself, Frédou was ordinarily the simplest of cats. He left scheming and tricks to lesser animals who needed such things to get by. Until the meeting with Thomasine, he had led a grandly straightforward existence. Dozing in the sunlight, prowling in the moonlight, fish, an occasional skirmish with a cat his size . . . that had been life for Frédou.

Now all was changed.

His mind seethed in the fashion of Madame Bobo's *pots au feu* in an effort to contrive some way to tempt Thomasine into living with him at the Montvert, and also to detach that Nameless One from her existence. Giving up his morning fish in order to remove the gray's thin appeal was a beginning. But it seemed to be taking a long time to fatten up the gray, who in any case was sly enough to look thin and starved whenever Thomasine's eyes were upon him. It was all a matter of attitude, whether one looked hungry or fed. A matter of attitude, that was, as long as one's stomach was full. Looking hungry when replete was simple, but looking fed when one was hungry took art. Frédou had found to his dismay that a life of easy living had blunted his ability as a hunter, and many times he had had to exercise his will not to cast longing eyes at Drummer's bone.

Moreover, the gray cat continued to slink nervously off whenever Frédou appeared in the courtyard of the house by Pont d'Arcole. This put Frédou in a rage, which only made Thomasine more sympathetic toward the smaller cat. On the point, once or twice, of explaining that the coward had just polished off Frédou's own breakfast— freely given him, which that gray very well knew, for all he kept up a pretense of getting the fish by stealth and daring—Frédou had realized each time that he'd only be defeating his own strategy.

So he had to continue in the role of a big agressor, while half the time he was starving because of his so-called victim, and Thomasine seemed no nearer to leaving that family of hers than she was on the day they met.

Until a few nights ago, Frédou had been able to think of no other scheme, and it was all so vexing that he was beginning to get thin just worrying about it.

And then one night—

81

He had left the Montvert late on a drizzly evening, making straight for the house of Thomasine. Detours to the Quai de Gesvres were for daytime. At this hour all the stores were closed, the birds shut inside, away from the view of admirers. Trotting along the wet streets, Frédou thought of the evil-tempered crow, who was undoubtedly longing for his home far away, just as that sullen little boy at the hotel was probably longing for his.

Frédou, who was devoted to his own home, the hotel where he had lived all his life, felt briefly sorry for these two aliens in Paris. But Thomasine, now . . . her he did not understand. She never actually had had a home. She traveled around the world in a wicker basket, lighting here, there, and everywhere, it seemed. Staying a month, a few weeks, climbing into the basket again, taking off. What sort of life was that for a cat, of all creatures the most settled?

On he hurried, stopping now and then to lick his paws free of wetness. Only for Thomasine would he have gone out on such a night. Even so, he paused once, gazing down on the Seine, where the lamplight from the bridges reflected shiveringly on the swift black waters, and wondered whether to turn back. There was a little door cut for him in the kitchen door, and in a matter of minutes he could be back and through it into the aromatic warmth. He could be on his cushion by the black, softly glowing stove.

Ah, but Thomasine . . .

And wouldn't the name of a Nameless One be there, even now, since in any case he had no place else in particular to go? There at her side, telling her lies about his prowess in stealing, and lies about the cruelty of Frédou?

No . . . he had to go on, rain or no rain.

Once he passed a gendarme walking firmly, white stick swinging, black raincoat glistening. The gendarme greeted him by name, and Frédou stopped for a moment to rub his flanks against the damp trousers, and mew a greeting. The gendarme

leaned over and scratched him properly, just behind the ears with a gentle pressure. Frédou
purred, and lashed his tail, and moved on.

Through deserted alleys and echoing archways
he went, past the great mysterious bulk of Notre
Dame, its towers lost in darkness, and so to the
house of his love.

In the courtyard the little fountain added the
sound of its tossing spray to that of the falling rain
and the rush of water through drainpipes. In black
depths the carp were hanging invisible, motion-
less. Ivy dripped on the walls. Crouched on the tile
roof, staring with wide wild eyes into the lighted
living room of Thomasine's temporary dwelling,
was the Nameless One. He turned at Frédou's soft
footfall, and, since there was no Thomasine to
watch, did not pretend to cower or quail.

"It's wet," he muttered.

"It always is, when it's raining," Frédou
growled, leaping to a wooden crate and thence to
the tiled roof, where he took his place beside the
gray and stared in turn at the scene within.

There she was, his cream and caramel beauty, stretched out beside a tiny leaping fire. *They* were there, too, disposed in chairs near the hearth, talking to each other, paying no heed to Thomasine. They could not, on the other hand, help heeding that Drummer, who kept drawing attention to himself in a shameless manner . . . thumping, wagging, barking.

"The only time," Frédou commented, "that a dog looks fulfilled is when he's with people. Otherwise, he just sits and waits for them to arrive. Have you ever noticed how empty a dog's eyes are when his owners are absent?"

"Isn't it beautiful?" said the gray, as if he hadn't heard. Frédou looked at Thomasine, who was lying on her side, lazily licking her chest, paying no attention either to Drummer or to *Them*. The Nameless One went on in a rapt way, "How wonderful they are. How kind, and handsome, and good."

"*They?*" said Frédou.

"And that dog, Drummer. Doesn't he look happy, and beloved? See how he prances, and carries that little ball, and flings himself at the man's feet. So sure of his welcome. So warm in there, with the lamps lit and that fire jumping up and down. I have never been near a fire, have you?"

"Oh, yes," said Frédou absently. He was beginning to get an idea, another solution. Only a glimmer as yet, but at least that. Ten minutes ago he'd had nothing but the interminable business of offering up his morning fish. "Thomasine," he said cautiously. "She looks lovely, wouldn't you say?"

"Hmm?" said the gray. "Oh, yes. Yes, everything in there is lovely. The people, the lights, the warmth, that dear fire—"

"And the dog," Frédou prompted.

"Certainly, the dog. He is part of it all."

"So is Thomasine."

"I'm not so sure," said the gray.

"What do you mean?"

"Well, she and I have had opportunities to talk—"

"I'm well aware of that," said Frédou.

The gray moved away slightly. "It has seemed to me—only seemed, you know, since I am young and understand as yet only death and hunger and fighting—that Thomasine is not really part of all this."

"And why do you say that?" Frédou asked warily, not allowing himself to take heart. As the gray said, he was young to know much of life yet, except what bitterness and wildness had taught him.

"Because she speaks haughtily of *Them*. Kindly, but without true warmth. She resents the wicker basket, and says sometimes she thinks traveling can be overdone. She says they're as restless as monkeys."

"Does she?" Frédou muttered. "Does she, indeed?"

"Of course," the gray went on, "she loves them. After all, they are the best and kindest and finest people in the world—"

"How do you know that?" said Frédou.

"One has only to look at them."

One has only, Frédou thought, to be hungry and wet and cold, and to think that *They* could provide an escape. This Nameless One, this thin gray son of a savage mother who'd never known the touch of a human hand, wanted to be a housecat, a pet. It was as simple as that.

Now, if somehow that could be turned to his, Frédou's, advantage?

The wise cat who'd seen hundreds of traveling people studied those two in the lighted room. Sleek, self-confident, hard-to-please. Their cat was a jewel, a princess among cats. Drummer, one had to admit, was a highly-bred dog. Whether or not one could stand him, one had to concede the breeding behind those long ears, those feathery legs, that shining fur.

Frédou turned his head a little and surveyed the cat beside him. Already an ear was faintly frayed from battle. No matter how you fed him, the fur would never be luxuriant, or any color but alley gray. The tail was hopeless, skinny and straight, lacking the patrician bend one observed in Thomasine's. *Those* people adopt *this* cat in place of Thomasine? It was laughable, and he was ten times a fool to have thought it for a second.

So much for that idea.

But Frédou was not easily defeated. He got up now, shook his paws one after the other, and, since clearly Thomasine was indoors for the night, made his departure without a sound. There was no need to trouble about the gray, who'd be around in the morning to conduct the farce of the fish.

Thinking hard, Frédou returned to his cushion by the black and glowing stove, where he curled up and dreamed of having Thomasine beside him, forever.

The very next morning he began to fix Paul with

his inviting yellow eyes, willing the boy to his side. He looked like the sort of boy who'd prefer dogs —privately Frédou thought this was true of all boys and it was perfectly agreeable to him—but on the other hand, he was clearly lonesome and cross, this boy. So what better time than this to win him to the idea of a cat for company? And what better cat, thought Frédou with simple pride, to achieve this end than the great Frédou himself?

For several mornings, as soon as the gray had absconded with his breakfast, Frédou lifted his eyes to the window where the boy was moping and invited him to come for a walk in beautiful Paris. He deferred his hunting, his nap, his own interests in every way, even to glimpses of Thomasine, in order to court Paul, who, he could see, began to take an interest, began to watch him curiously, as though scarcely believing that Frédou could actually desire his company.

Then those other ones, his parents, went away and left the boy to himself, and that very morning Frédou was gratified to see the boy appear at the kitchen door and eye him wonderingly, waiting to see—

Frédou stood, yawned, walked deliberately to Paul's side, gazed up at him commandingly, and then set slowly off upon a walk, looking back to be sure that Paul was following.

SEVEN

Two mornings later, when Mr. and Mrs. Roberts returned from their trip to Versailles, they looked in their son's room and found him gone.

"Ah, yes," said Monsieur Picot, who had accompanied them upstairs, "unquestionably he is off with Frédou once again."

"Off with Frédou?" said Mr. Roberts. "How's that?"

"Your fine little grouchy boy, who is no longer so much of a grouch, has taken to the company of Monsieur Frédou. Every morning now they set off together, to explore the sights of Paris, I take it."

"But . . . but maybe he'll get lost," Mrs. Roberts protested.

"Have no fear," said Monsieur Picot. "Frédou at all times knows exactly what he is doing."

"I didn't mean Frédou."

"He will guard the boy like a kitten of his own, take my word for it. Of course," Monsieur Picot added, touching his mustaches, "no one of us knows just *why* Frédou displays this sudden interest in a boy. He has never, but *never*, cared for any person except our late employer, God rest her. Still . . . that is how it has turned out. Frédou seems to fancy Paul, and Paul perhaps likes Frédou, and perhaps is just glad to have an animal to walk with again. He tells me he walks a great deal with his dog."

"Oh, he does," said Mrs. Roberts. "He and Aladdin are constantly together. But he's never seemed to care much for cats before. Of course," she added, "he did take to that kitten in the Pantheon. But Frédou is hardly a hungry-looking kitten."

"Hardly," said Monsieur Picot, who was exceedingly proud of Frédou, if a little jealous of him. "You will see a marvelous change, I assure you, in your little boy. Marvelous. All wrought by Frédou."

When the concierge had gone, Mr. and Mrs. Roberts looked at each other and smiled.

"He certainly has a lot of faith in that cat," said Mr. Roberts.

"Doesn't he, though," said Mrs. Roberts, and added, "I wish Paul would come back, just the same. I'm not sure he's safe, even with the mighty

Frédou. After all, Paris is a big city, and he is rather a small boy."

She need not have concerned herself, for Frédou never went too far from the hotel. He had his radius of wandering, limited to the Latin Quarter, the Ile St. Louis and the Ile de la Cité. Within these

confines he could not get lost, and outside them he did not allow Paul to go.

For his part, Paul was happy just to follow where the big cat led. In only three mornings he had come to know many people. The Turkish baker across the street from the hotel, the rug peddler with his golden ear-hoops, the fruit man and the flower woman all greeted Paul in the morning now as if he'd lived near them all his life. To each he said a grave *bonjour*, and even added a couple of other words in French. *"Très bien,"* he'd say, and then, seeing they'd been the right words, would add, *"Très, très bien."* And all would smile and beam upon him. His face lost its worried frown, and without noticing it, he started to be happy.

This morning he was following Frédou in an aimless fashion, forgetting that his parents were due home. He looked with alert eyes at all the sights he'd refused, till now, to see—at the chestnut trees gently rustling along the banks of the

Seine, and at the fishermen sitting patiently on the embankment, their lines in the dark water; at the flutter of awnings, the glitter of coffee urns in the cafés, the brightness of flowers everywhere. Priests zoomed by on motorbikes, black garments streaming behind them, heads helmeted like racers. Workers in blue smocks went along the sidewalks, whistling cheerfully. With fleet and fancy gestures gendarmes controlled the traffic, and in the market streets Paul walked over lettuce leaves and sniffed the wonderful odors . . . coffee, bread, cheeses, and onion soup. The sky was high and blue and spattered with flecks of cottony clouds, the air sunny, spicy, tossed by a quick breeze.

Paul, breathing deeply, looking around with eager eyes, decided that after all Paris was pretty nice. Not home, but nice.

"Voulez-vous acheter des fleurs, monsieur?"

Paul stared in surprise at a little girl, barefoot, dirty, pretty, who stared up at him and waved a

bunch of violets under his nose. She was calling *him* Monsieur? He stared around, looked back at the girl, and realized that she really, actually, was.

Now, what had she said? Well, obviously, would he buy these violets. She had a little tray of them under one thin arm, and she jingled a few coins in the pocket of her loose, frayed, very dirty dress.

Feeling old, feeling completely grown up and rich and powerful, Paul took a good-sized coin from his pocket and handed it to the girl. Apparently it was enough. Maybe more than, he thought with a grin, because she thrust the violets at him, dashed away a few steps, turned and blew him a kiss, and then ran on her swift, shoeless, completely dirty feet, through the crowds, and was gone.

Paul sniffed the violets and sighed, and turned without thinking, or looking for Frédou, back toward the hotel. He hadn't known that he knew the way, but he did. He forgot Frédou. For almost the first time since leaving America, he stopped longing for home and Aladdin. In some way he could not easily explain to himself, he was even glad now to think that Aladdin was having a happy summer at the beach. Though it was too much to be glad that Turkey Hoffman was having it with him.

He retraced his steps thoughtfully, and found,

at the hotel, his parents, returned from Versailles. Not knowing what else to do with them, he gave the violets to his mother, and then was ashamed because she was so pleased to think he'd bought her a present. It was his first experience with the rather nervous joys of undeserved praise.

They said the trip to Versailles had been most successful, and wasn't he sorry now that he hadn't gone along?

"Not very," said Paul, being exceedingly honest about this in order to make up for not being honest about the violets. "I had a good time here."

"You do seem the better for a couple of days on your own," said his father. "Monsieur Picot says you've been wandering about with Frédou. Does he make a good escort?"

Paul gasped. "Oh, gosh," he said. "I went and forgot all about him. I mean, I just walked away and left him."

"I imagine he's capable of finding his way home," said Mr. Roberts.

Paul thought Frédou capable of anything. "Oh, sure," he said, relaxing. "He'll be fine."

"Gotten mighty fond of him, haven't you?" Mr. Roberts said.

Paul hesitated. The truth was, that though in the company of Frédou he'd enjoyed this summer in a way he hadn't thought possible, he had *not* gotten very fond of him. In some strange way, Frédou was just not a cat a person could get very fond of. Maybe too proud, or too sure of himself, too *apart*. He didn't join with you, the way a dog did. He wasn't in the least cuddly, hardly even friendly. Paul had felt privileged to be allowed to rub Frédou's ears once or twice. A nice cat, Paul thought, trying to be loyal. After all, he had had a fine time with Frédou. He no longer felt sulky, and that, surely, was because he'd gone out and looked at things and talked to people and even begun to speak French. And who was responsible for it all except Frédou?

"He's a very nice cat," he said, "only, nobody's pet."

The violets didn't last the day. By afternoon they had shriveled into damp little purple rags hanging on limp stems. Mrs. Roberts pressed a few of them in a guidebook to Paris and regretfully threw the rest away. Paul was sorry, too, in a way, to see them go. He thought he would always remember that pretty little girl with her dirty face and feet, waving the bunch of violets under his nose. As a matter of fact, he always did.

The next morning he was sitting at his window, wondering whether or not to go walking with Frédou again, and rather thinking he wouldn't, when his mother came into his room and asked whether he'd like to go on a boat ride on the Seine with them in the evening.

"We can have dinner on the boat, and see the lights go on along the river, and it should be lots of fun," she said. "Your father wants to get the tickets this morning."

"Sure, I'd love it," said Paul.

It certainly was pleasant, getting along with people. Somehow it not only made you feel better, but made the other people nicer, too. His father didn't seem stern now, and his mother wasn't going about with that disappointd look on her face. Peculiar, thought Paul, already forgetting how hard he had been to get along with, only remembering that his parents had been.

"Hey," he said, "look down there." His mother came to stand beside him at the window.

In the courtyard below, Yvette was doing the blue wash in the wooden tub. Sitting on the tile table, watching her idly, was Frédou, beside his fish. As Paul had spoken, the gray cat came peering around a corner and now was pursuing his stealthy approach toward the breakfast he'd come to expect.

"Now, watch," said Paul to his mother. "It's the funniest thing. That gray cat will sneak up to the table and hook Frédou's fish, and big old Frédou won't do a thing about it. I think he's *afraid* of that little cat."

"Really?" said Mrs. Roberts, leaning forward to

see better. "Why Paul, how can you say that?"

For Frédou, waiting until the thin gray cat was almost within reach of the prize, turned suddenly, fur standing on end, so that he looked as big as a fox, his mouth wide and snarling. He lunged terribly at the gray, who, after one desperate last swipe at the fish, ran up the wall of the toolshed as if it were a tree and crouched on the roof, trembling.

"Why, that *bully*," Paul shouted. "Did you see that? How he attacked that little tiny cat, that—"

"Well, Paul," said Mrs. Roberts. "It *is* Frédou's fish, after all. He has to protect it. Would Aladdin give up a bone to another dog?"

"Aladdin," Paul said firmly, "would never attack a small little hungry animal. Never. I bet—I bet Aladdin would like that cat. That little gray one. He looks sort of like the cat in Rome, doesn't he?"

"Now, just a second, Paul," said Mrs. Roberts, but her son had already gone running down the snail stairway, through the curtain of wooden beads, the parlor, the hall, the kitchen—where Madame Bobo, in her astonishment, dropped an egg on the floor—and into the courtyard, where Frédou was munching on his fish with calm satisfaction, and Yvette was laughing as she turned the hose into the tub, and the gray cat was shivering on the shed roof.

"Kitty, kitty, kitty . . ." said Paul, approaching the shed. "Nice little gray kitty—" He stretched out his hand, to let the small cat sniff at it. For a moment it seemed that the gray would flee again. He laid his ears down, backed a few steps, and crouched again, green eyes glittering, then cautiously, slowly, stretched his neck forward. The nose, black as a truffle, wrinkled. Paul remained absolutely still as the little cat, finding he couldn't reach the hand, inched forward.

Nose touched finger, the cat sprang backward, flattened, and the whole ballet began again. Four times the small gray advanced, retreated, in this,

his first human contact. All the while Paul, with the patience of one who has trained a puppy, waited quietly. Yvette, the hose limp in her hand, watched fascinated. Madame Bobo came to the door to observe. Mr. and Mrs. Roberts leaned from Paul's window to see.

Frédou, one possessive paw across his fish, followed every move.

Ten minutes later, the gray cat, in purring ecstasy, was nestled in Paul's arms, and Mr. and Mrs. Roberts were resigning themselves to taking a French cat back to Long Island.

In the days that followed, the Nameless One, now called Bobo-Yvette-Marie-Pierre-Picot (Bobo, for short) took to the role of pet the way the carp took to the waters of the pool, or those birds on the Quai de Gesvres had once taken to the air. He submitted to a bath, ate anything that was given him, slept at the foot of Paul's bed, and came at the sound of Paul's voice from anywhere. And when at last he was in America, he learned to play with Aladdin, to sit by the fire, to appropriate laps to his own use. He felt, in every way, as lucky as he had once found Thomasine to be. Frédou had been right. This thin gray son of a savage mother had wanted, not Thomasine, but Thomasine's home life. He had wanted to be a pet, and he made a very good one.

EIGHT

Thomasine, on the other hand, gave up everything Bobo had wanted. She exchanged the hearth for a kitchen stove, her lamplit cozy evenings for prowls through the deserted courtyards and echoing archways of Paris at night, her cooked shrimp and chicken livers for a raw fish beside Frédou. In time she was less of a pet even than Frédou–who, after

111

all, would permit a gendarme to scratch his ears, providing it was done properly.

It happened this way—

When Paul had left the courtyard, carrying the blissful gray in his arms, Frédou finished off his fish in a meditative way. He was perplexed at how simple things turned out to be. Here he'd been starving, missing Thomasine, walking till his paws bled with that clearly dog-loving boy, all to win the boy to a love of cats, when it appeared that none of it had been necessary. The only thing necessary had been to arouse the boy's defensiveness for a small animal. And this Frédou had done entirely by accident, and only because this morning he'd been too hungry, at last, to give up his fish.

Well, thought Frédou, excusing himself, it was difficult to know what went on in the minds of people. Particularly in the minds of boys.

He finished breakfast—his first in days—performed a prolonged and luxurious toilet there in the sun on the warm tile table. He could not, of course, be sure what would happen now, but thought it safe to consider that gray out of the picture, so far as Thomasine was concerned. If Frédou was any judge of life, and he rather felt he was, that Nameless One would presently not only have a name, but would be so well fed he wouldn't have a rib to offer Thomasine's brooding eye. *If* he ever went back to the house by Pont d'Arcole again, which was doubtful. Why go and peer in a window at the joys of home life when you could have them for yourself?

The gray would have a name, and be richly fed, and be established here at the hotel for as long as those people stayed. Which wouldn't, Frédou assured himself contentedly, be long. People never did stay here for long.

With one tremendous yawn, followed by a leisurely stretch—front legs, then back—Frédou leaped lightly to the ground and set off for Pont d'Arcole. He scarcely heard the greetings of the bookstall keepers, did not stop to nibble at rose leaves, and left the Quai de Gesvres for another day. He wanted to find Thomasine. Today it did not even matter so much that he persuade her to his way. He merely wanted to see her great blue eyes and hear her husky voice and watch the sinuous motion of that incomparable tail.

Arriving at the leafy courtyard, he could find no trace of her. He sprang to the jutting roof where so often he and the gray had sat together, each gazing upon what he desired, but the great room was empty.

Still—there was a change of some sort. Frédou sat, puzzled, looking at boxes and trunks, at sheet-covered furniture. Then, in a disagreeable flash of knowledge, he realized what was going on. *They*, the restless ones, were preparing to move on once more. *And to take with them his beautiful Thomasine.* That basket there—that big wicker basket with the lid thrown back—must be the very one she'd spoken of. No cat, of course, minded getting in a box or a basket. Such places could be cozy and comfortable. But to be thrust into one bodily! The indignity of it made Frédou shudder.

But where, oh, where, was Thomasine?

"Frédou," came a low voice, her voice, from the bushes. "Frédou, come down here. Only do not let them see where you go."

Frédou looked all around, then light as a shadow sped to the side of Thomasine, huddled under a laurel, out of sight.

"*They're* after me," she said.

"Aren't they always?"

"I mean, they plan another trip."

"They always plan another trip. They'll be planning another trip forever, and taking you with them, round and round, all over the world, forever," he growled.

"Oh, no, Frédou. I've changed my mind. I do not wish to go with them anymore. Except—"

"Except?" prompted Frédou, overjoyed and uneasy at once. "Except, what?"

"Well, they have been so good to me . . . so kind. They will miss me so terribly."

Frédou said, "*I* am the one who would miss you. *They* will look around, and sigh a little, and say whatever could have happened, and then they'll get another cat. It's what people always do."

"You," said Thomasine, "do not really know much about people at all, do you?"

"No," he admitted. "But I do know about cats," he went on, "and I know that my fish and my stove and myself are yours, if you will come with me."

Thomasine looked uncertain. She studied Frédou with her sapphire eyes, and said suddenly, "But Frédou, you look so *thin*."

Frédou started to say that was perfectly all right, his days of starvation were over, when he thought that perhaps it would be wiser not to explain anything. All at once he looked even thinner and hungrier. He grew gaunt before her eyes. It wasn't only the gray knew tricks like that, and if a hungry look was the way to win Thomasine, he was prepared to look hungry all the rest of his life.

He could not help, at the same time, looking proud. He was, after all, Frédou. And Thomasine, gazing at this wonder, knew she could not leave with *Them*, no matter how kind, how good, they were. They were people, she was a cat. And Frédou the very cat of cats.

"*And that*," said Thomasine, "*is that.*"

Without a backward glance at the garden, the fountain, the house where she had lived and been perfectly happy—almost perfectly happy—she set off at the side of Frédou, and never, after that, left it.

In one thing Frédou was wrong. *They* knew just what had happened. The man, standing at the window, said to the woman, "Thomasine is eloping with that big apricot devil who's been hanging around here day and night."

"Shall we go after her?" the woman asked.

The man sighed. He was very fond of Thomasine. "No," he said at last. "Let her go. She'll be happier with him."

Drummer, who was delighted at the whole turn of events, wagged his tail in agreement.

Before Mr. and Mrs. Roberts and Paul left with their pet, Bobo, for America, Mr. Roberts took two pictures of Monsieur and Madame Picot and all the staff. One picture to hang in the lobby over the spider fern, and one to hang in the parlor where all could see.

"What a pity," wailed Monsieur Picot, "that Frédou and his beautiful friend are not here to be included in the photograph."

"You can't find them?" said Mr. Roberts.

"Monsieur, I have searched in vain."

Frédou and Thomasine, who were not interested in having their picture taken, were far away, in a little park at the very tip of the Ile St. Louis. They were sitting side by side in the shade of a plane tree, watching the boats go up and down the Seine. As they watched, Thomasine told Frédou stories of the world she had traveled over for so long. Frédou, with all his curiosity to satisfy, listened contentedly.

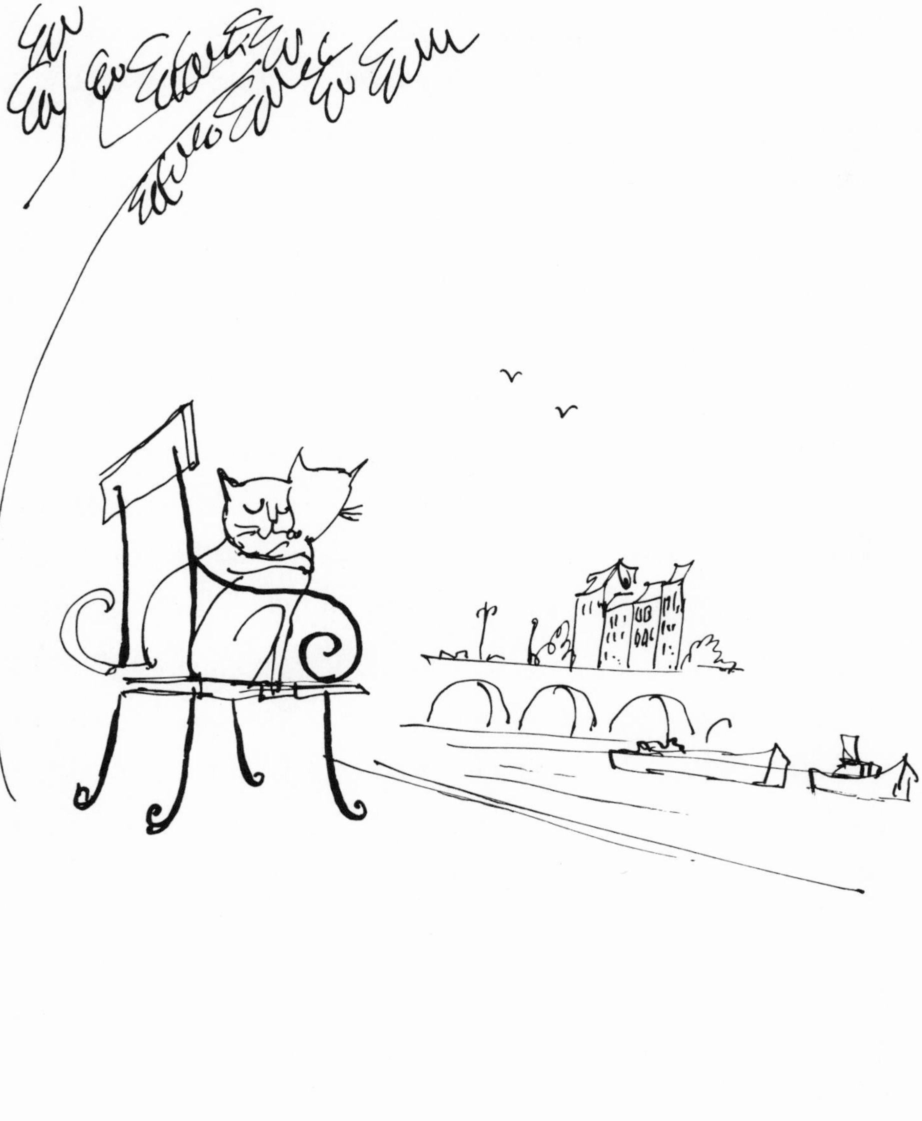

Set in Linotype Baskerville

Format by Jean Krulis

Set by The Haddon Craftsmen, Inc.

Printed by the Murray Printing Co.

Bound by Haddon Bindery

Published by HARPER & BROTHERS, *New York*